How Santa and His Reindeer Came to Fly

A Touch from Christ Made Santa's Reindeer Fly

JG Matyas

WestBow Press books may be ordered through booksellers or by contacting:

WestBow Press
A Division of Thomas Nelson & Zondervan
1663 Liberty Drive
Bloomington, IN 47403
www.westbowpress.com
1 (866) 928-1240

Because of the dynamic nature of the Internet, any web addresses or links contained in this book may have changed since publication and may no longer be valid. The views expressed in this work are solely those of the author and do not necessarily reflect the views of the publisher, and the publisher hereby disclaims any responsibility for them.

Any people depicted in stock imagery provided by Getty Images are models, and such images are being used for illustrative purposes only. Certain stock imagery © Getty Images.

Scripture taken from The Jerusalem Bible © 1966, 1968 by Darton Longman & Todd Ltd and Doubleday and Company Ltd. All rights reserved.

This is a work of fiction. All of the characters, names, incidents, organizations, and dialogue in this novel are either the products of the author's imagination or are used fictitiously.

ISBN: 978-1-9736-5703-3 (sc)
ISBN: 978-1-9736-5704-0 (e)

Library of Congress Control Number: 2019903049

Print information available on the last page.

WestBow Press rev. date: 04/26/2019

WESTBOW
PRESS®
A DIVISION OF THOMAS NELSON
& ZONDERVAN

DEDICATION

I dedicate this story to my Heavenly Father, His Son and the Spirit as one; to my earthly family, our parents who are now gone but especially to my wife, Kathleen who without her support this poem may have never been written; and to our four daughters: Kate, Becki, Sarah and Susan and their children: Camryn, Zachary, Clayton, Taylor, Brady, Cannon, Hayley, Sayla, Michael and Jaime for without their support this book would never have been published.

May these words be a reminder that the mystery of Christmas Spirit magic comes directly from the finger of Christ. So as Dickens' character, Tiny Tim last observed, "God Bless us, every one."

PREFACE

How Santa and His reindeer came to fly

I was dreaming about the beginning of time,

when the cosmos was deep, dark, dense and sublime;

then nothing became something as an image of Eternal Light,

when that something was given a spark of knowing wrong from right;

this Eternal Light within infinity first imparted sense to darkness,

then darkness gave meaning to the Light with these words "I AM WHO

I AM" (Exodus 3:14)*

giving life to new spirits of angels and man

yet, creation raises a question of Obedience?

In my dream, the answer was silence followed by an unbelievable action,

disobedience!

Then the Light of my dream screamed forth a thunder, If True Love

raises this question then is more True Love the answer?

What the Eternal Light had begun will be made new again but only now

under perfect control of its Master.

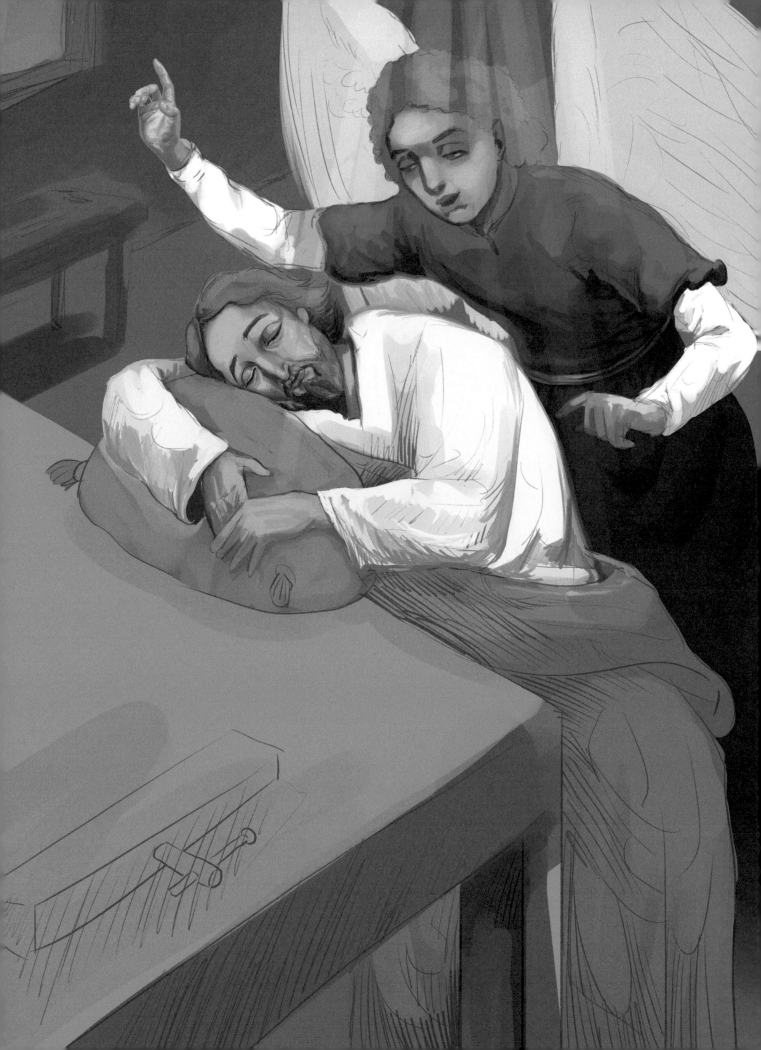

THIS IS A STORY OF SANTA, A SPIRIT OF CHRIST'S LOVE

In a small village of Nazareth was a man From David's House

Selected through the prayers of the temple Joseph was chosen Mary's spouse

To take hold of, honor and be her protector

Was counseled by an angel not to disappoint or reject her.

A vessel before him contains the word and the flame

Redemption begins with the sound of her name.

Take heed, the king needs a counting for taxes owed

Yet render to Caesar what is his, in silver and gold.

Treasure on earth while coins of the realm

Takes Joseph and Mary to the city of Bethlehem

Holy Grail was carried on a burro tonight

Guarded and protected by angles in flight;

Joseph with Mary were wed to the mission

Committed to complete once they gave their permission

Five days was their journey, it was a climb up the hill

Arriving in Nazareth in cold night air chill.

No room for this couple No place to rest and sleep

Bed down on the floor on hay near some sheep

Joseph fed the donkey, stored their gear, and knelt with Mary to pray

Much about to happen in the center of this cave.

Bright Light, Star Light Good News unfolds

A New True Light is dawning the Messiah foretold;

Prophets let it be written, now let it be done,

Our God in the Heavens has sent forth His Son.

A covenant established and a promise now fulfilled,

Salvation this reason on which God will rebuild.

Michael the Archangel announces it loud and clear

Heaven acknowledges our Christ child is here

Let all be on notice, Let all not ignore

God's rescue starts now repairing man's error

No longer will man be grieving no longer will he be lost

What begins in a wooden manger will finish on a wooden cross.

Step into this stable, step onto the cave floor.

The Heavens have opened sending prophets to praise and adore.

There was Moses, Abraham, David, and Isaiah from the past

But those heavenly spirits were not the entire cast.

Near Joseph kneeling in reverence was a spirit of sorts

Unseen to all except the other Spirits of course,

His headdress removed, his head bowed to the floor

Was a vision of a future Churchman, who too came to adore

In truth, this is a vision in the form of a man, who is poised to inspire a

Traditional celebration, his name will be known as the Bishop of Myra.

It happens you see that Nicholas was there

When four small fawn drawn by angels to the stable to stare

at a twinkling light above an animal food trough

attracted each fawn to move in just a bit closer and not wander off

so close that a touch from the babe's finger excited a new history

and with it Our Father created a fulfilling Christmas mystery

From that very moment as night cleared the sky

A touch from a finger of Jesus helped Santa Claus fly

Tonight brings the gift of salvation to the souls of all men

This gift gives faith to the hopeless, brings poor charity, a part of God's plan

Now True Light begets His word in swaddling form

The greatest gesture of love our Father transforms

Now a bolt of light from this child is a transfer of sorts

Gives fuel to the fire and power to St. Nick's cohorts

Remember the poor, the needy and forgotten

Remember to appreciate and share those gifts you've gotten

Make a gesture or a smile and maybe shed a tear

Pray for those present, family and friends who were once here.

Now lay your head down on a pillow tonight

Listen for sleigh bells look for lighted reindeer in flight

While a jolly white haired man in a red suit may appear

Christ's graces fuel the flight, lights the way for his bright lighted reindeer.

Most say it is better to give gifts then to receive

Charity is the wrapping on this solemn Holy Day we all call Christmas Eve.

Epilogue

Love no longer questioned since True Love is God's answer.

Christmas is that Season and it lives forever after.

Give praise to our God for sending the Light;

And praise to the Spirit who carries the Light;

And praise to the Son for all He has done;

And praise for words He puts on man's tongue.

Mankind who looks toward the sun to brighten each day,

Will now look to God's Son to show man His way.

The birth of this child is just a beginning,

It starts a whole process forgiving man's sinning.

Christ's light confirms His Father's word and fulfills His Father's story.

A Messiah was promised, prophesized and now proclaims all God's glory.

Faith in The Christ enlightens the past while nourishing hope in the future

God's gift of True Light extends His hand in a pure loving gesture

God presents Jesus as His True gift and the reason we gift our family and friends.

God has established this Christmas Spirit to be with man until the end.

While Christ's birth is the true reason and the crux of this story,

A jolly old bishop and reindeer exist to remind generations of His eternal glory.

Take note all who see stars streak through the Christmas Eve sky.

A finger from Christ's hand made Santa's sleigh and reindeer fly.

Wood from a manger is the same wood of a cross.

So Look to our Spirits for repair of our earthly loss.

Failure has no option, failure only can lead to a fall.

If change fails to work there may be nothing at all;

I AM never fails, I AM makes no flaws

HIS representatives are required to follow HIS law.

So a new woman and a new man were selected to show

That once and for all I AM is in control.

AMEN

About the Author

A husband to Kathleen, a father of four daughters and a grandfather of eight. Catholicism has been the basis of his religious education; raised by Byzantine Catholic parents, educated from elementary through College by Franciscans, Marist Brothers and Benedictines.